바람이

달다

—

ART IS
LIFE

처음 시작하는 마음으로 정성스럽게 책을 보고 작업하자.
아무것도 아는 것이 없다, 너는. 무지無知에서 출발하자.

바람이

달다

―

서정자 글, 그림

지식공감

PROLOGUE

2016년 11월 29일, 뉴욕에서 열 번째 개인전을 마무리하면서 지나간 시간들을 생각해 보았다.

겁 없이 붓을 들었던 20대 초반부터 50대가 된 지금까지, 난 나의 작업을 한번 정리하고 싶었다.

여기 실린 글들은 내 작업 노트에 드문드문 적혀 있던 나의 일상이 고스란히 담긴 것들이다.

간혹 부족해 보이는 것도 있지만, 첫 느낌 그대로 수정 없이 나의 책 『바람이 달다』를 만들었다.

우리의 삶이 늘 따뜻한 봄날처럼 맑을 수는 없을지라도, 때론 비바람 불고 마음이 시린 날, 오랜 친구의 낡은 노트를 펼쳐본 것처럼 이 책이 작은 위로와 희망과 열정이 되어 주었으면 좋겠다.

이 모든 것은 사랑하는 나의 가족이 있었기에 가능했다.

– 2017년 봄, 작업실에서 **서정자**

On 29th November, 2016, I reminisced about the passing moments while wrapping up the tenth solo exhibition held in New York. I have always wanted to organized my works from my early twenties when I was bold and had no fear of taking out my brush to my fifties together. The writings in this book are my daily which have been described in parts of my work notes. The writings may be unsophisticated, however, I decided to write my first book 'The wind is sweet' without any dramatization in order to deliver my first raw feelings to you.

Although our lives can't always be as clear as warm spring day, I hope that this book can be a little bit of comfort, hope, and enthusiasm. All of this was possible because I had my family in love beside me.

- **Seo Jeong-Ja** in studio in spring, 2017

CONTENTS | 차례

PART 1

"흰색은 모든 가능성으로 가득한 침묵"

"White is silence full of all possibilities."

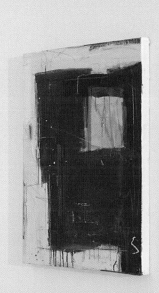

01 | White & White 06. 60 x 72cm Mixed media on canvas. 2006

01

그림을 그리는 행위는 시간과의 싸움이다. 그 시간들의 흔적이 쌓여서 작품의 화면이 되고 공간감이 이루어진다.

나의 작업은 수많은 시간이 채워졌다 지워졌다 하는 반복의 행위이다.

그 반복의 행위 속에서 마티에르(matière)가 자연스럽게 생겨나고, 상생과 소멸의 시간이 들어가게 된다.

절제된 드로잉, 절제된 컬러, 백지가 가진 흰색을 칸딘스키는 "흰색은 모든 가능성으로 가득한 침묵"이라고 표현했다.

채우기보다 비워내는 작업, 물질보다는 정신, 형상보다는 비형상.

나는 오랫동안 직선의 그 날카롭고 간결함을 사랑해왔다.

사각 공간은 어떤 대상과 대상의 상호 호흡과 흐름, 소통의 장이라고 생각해왔다. 그 차가움의 공간에 색을 입히고 여러 가지 표현을 하고 더 깊은 공간감으로 느림과 쉼표의 미학으로 표현하고자 한다.

창작이란 창조가 아닌 발견이라고 했다. 그 발견의 흔적을 찾아서 여행을 떠나보면 어떨까 한다.

– 서정자 작업 일지 중에서

Act of painting is a battle against time. Those moments in time are stacked up to form the picture and create the impression of space.

My work involves the repetitive act of time filling up and erasing.

From the act of repetition, Martière naturally occurs co-existence and extinction comes into time.

Kandisky expressed white as "a deep, absolute silence, full of possibility."

Works emptying out rather than filling in, spiritual rather than material, and intangible rather than tangible.

I have loved the sharpness and simplicity of straight lines for a long time.

Rectangular space has been thought as a field of mutual breathing, flow, and communication between objects. I intend to fill the cold space with colors, describe it in various forms, and express the space with more depth via the aesthetics of slowness and comma.

Creative work is rather a discovery than a creation. I plan on going on a trip to seek for trace of the discovery.

- From daily workbooks of **Seo Jeong Ja**

02 | Untitled 227 x 182cm Mixed media on canvas. 2001

세상이라는 사유의 공간.

안개 낀 새벽빛은 암갈색.

깊어가는 밤하늘은 청회색.

계절에 따라서 하나하나 달라진다.

공기도, 빛의 느낌도, 우리의 호흡도.

그림도 그때그때 시간의 흐름에 따라 달라진다.

흐름에 따라서 달라지는 채색.

계속 쌓여가는 마티에르.

시간은 쌓는 것이다.

그 흔적들을 남기는 것이다.

결국, 그림은 그때그때의 다큐멘터리인 것이다.

—

The world is Space for thinking.

Misty dawn light is burnt umber.

Deepening night sky is slate grey.

Everything changes one by one as the seasons go by.

So does the air, the sense of light, and even our breath.

The painting also changes depending on the flow of time.

Changes in coloration with flow

Continuously-accumulating Matiere.

It is to leave the trace.

At the end, paintings are documentaries at every moment.

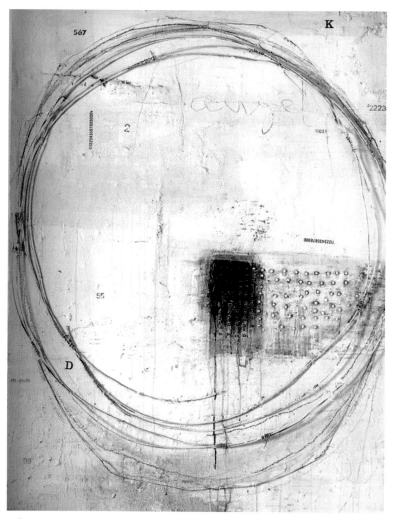

03 | Untitled 163 x 130cm Mixed media on canvas. 2001

바람이 불어온다.

투명한 햇살이 묻어오는 것을 보니 곧 봄이 가까이 왔다.

겨울의 끄트머리에 부는 바람은 다디단 냄새가 난다.

언뜻언뜻 추위, 꽃샘추위가 있지만

그 바람은 대지에서 생명이 춤추는, 바로 생명이 잉태된…

그래서 단 냄새가 난다.

—

The wind rises.

As the shiny sunlight lays upon, I notice spring is nearby.

The wind that blows in the edge of late winter smells sweet.

From time to time, there is a wave of the last cold spell

However, the wind is life dancing on the earth where the life is newly born...

Thus, the wind smells so sweet.

04 | Untitled 79 x 91cm Mixed media on canvas. 2001

흰색, 그리고 검은색.

철저하게 반대의 색이다.

서로의 겸허함으로 완벽해지는 색이다.

우리도 누군가에게 겸허해지기 위해서는 나를 낮추어야 한다.

낮아져야만 더 겸허해진다.

그 겸허함 속에 진실과 자유가 존재한다.

그러할 때 더 잘 보이게 된다.

그리고 배려의 마음이 생긴다.

서로를 겸허하게 이해하게 된다.

—

White and black.

They are perfectly contrasting colors.

Through mutual humility, the two colors become perfect.

In order to show humility to other, we also need to lower ourselves.

Only when we lower ourselves, we can truly become humbler.

In such humility exists the truth and freedom.

Then, we can see it more clearly and become more considerate to others.

05
—

작업실에서 우두커니,

조용하게 그냥 앉아 있는 시간이 많다.

딱히 뭘 하지도 않지만,

온전히 나를 비우면서 필요 없는 생각을 버리는 시간.

그 시간은 나에게 무척 중요한 시간이다.

—

When I am in studio,

I have enough space to contemplate quietly.

It is a time for me to empty myself

and get rid of unnecessary thoughts.

Those moments are extremely crucial.

05 | White & White 0603. 150 x 120cm Mixed media on canvas. 2006

06 | Untitled 162 x 130cm Mixed media on canvas. 1998

06

종종 그림이 내게 말을 걸어올 때가 있다.

그럴 때면 그저 무심하게 그림을 바라본다.

나를 표현해 줘서 고마워요.

나에게로 와줘서 고맙다.

—

There are times when the paintings talk to me.

I look at them indifferently.

"Thank you for painting me."

Thank you for coming.

07 | Untitled 194 x 260cm Mixed media on canvas. 1999

나의 작업은 무수한 물질들로 구성되어 있다.
낡은 철판과 나무와 스티로폼…
미묘한 색조 변화와 오브제들을
하나의 호흡으로…

My works are composed of numerous materials.
Old iron plates, woods, Styrofoam…
Subtle color changes and objects
In harmony tune…

우리는 사랑하면 알게 된다고 한다.

시간이 조금 흘러간 후에,

무심하게 그린 그림이 참 따스하게 느껴질 때가 있다.

옛날에는 그림이 마음에 들지 않아서,

많이 찢어 버리고는 했었다.

하나 지금은 잠시 숨을 고르고,

며칠 후에 다시 그 그림을 보고 있자면

전혀 다른 느낌이 와 닿고는 한다.

—

When we fall in love, we come to know each other.

After some time has passed,

Time to time, I feel the warmth in the paintings that I indifferently painted in the past.

In the old days, I would often tear up those painting which I thought unimpressive.

But now, I take a moment before doing so.

When I look at those painting again after couple of days, the paintings come to be from a different perspective.

08 | White & White 0607. 120 x 150cm Mixed media on canvas. 2006

09 | Untitled 73 x 61cm Mixed media on canvas. 2004

작업실의 공간.

온갖 물감이 떨어져 있는 바닥은 지저분하다.

그냥 세월의 흔적이라고 생각하자.

벌써 이곳에서 14년째…

—

My Studio.

The floor is messy with smudges of colorful paints.

Let's just call it as trace of time.

It has already been 14 years.

차를 한잔 우려내는 시간은 나에게 참 소중하다.

차를 한잔 우려내고 있으면, 맑아지는 차와 같이

내 몸과 마음이 정화되고는 한다.

이 의식이 나를 다시 생각하게 만든다.

—

Those moments preparing for a cup of tea is very precious to me.

As I brew the tea, I feel like my body

and soul are being cleansed like the clear tea.

This ritual makes me think again.

10 | Untitled 163 x 130cm Mixed media on canvas. 1999

11 | Untitled 194 x 260cm Mixed media on canvas. 1999

11

좋은 작품이란 어떤 것일까?
아름다움의 궁극의 목표는,
처절한 아름다움은
한참 꽃이 필 때가 아닌
꽃이 지고 난 후 그 외로움이 겹칠 때
발현되는 것이 아닐까.

—

What does it really mean by a good work?

The absolute beauty emerges

not when the flowers bloom,

but rather when the flowers fall

and loneliness is overlapped.

12
—

그저 웅덩이처럼 가만히 고여 있어서는,
썩어가는 수밖에 없다.
흐르는 강물처럼, 계곡처럼,
우리는 끊임없이 고민하며 흘러가야만 한다.
고민이 없으면 발전도 없다.

—

Stagnant water tends to rot.
Like a flowing river and valley,
we must constantly think and move.
Without thinking, there is no more improvement.

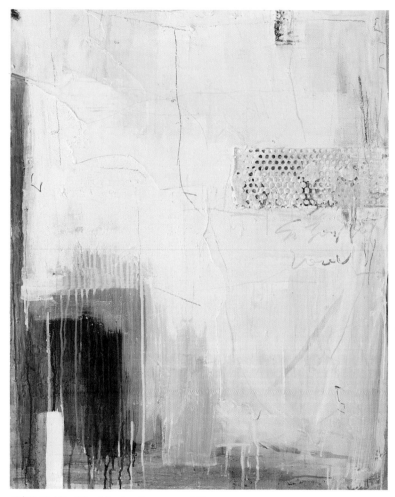

13 | Untitled 91 x 117cm Mixed media on canvas. 2001

13
—

맑은 그림을 그리고 싶다.

어떠한 사람이건 내 그림으로써 삶의 치유를 받을 수 있도록,

누군가는 내 그림을 보고 영혼이 맑아질 수 있도록.

—

I want to draw a pure painting.

So that anyone can heal one's life and

So that someone can brighten one's soul through my paintings.

14 | Untitled 46 x 53cm Mixed media on canvas. 2002

시간은 모든 것을 간직한다.

오래된 사원의 벽과,

오래된 시간의 의미.

어쩌면 카르마,

친숙한 바람 냄새.

이 순간의 기다림이 있었기에

나는 지금 여기에 머물러 있다.

—

Time cherishes everything.

The walls of the old temple

The meaning of old time

Maybe, it's karma.

Familiar smell of the wind.

Because of this moment of waiting

I am staying here now.

15 | White & White 0601. 520 x 193cm Mixed media on canvas. 2006

15
—

눈물은 우리에게 위안을 준다.

울고 나면 모든 것이 달라져 보인다.

맑은 눈물, 영혼의 치유제.

—

Tears give us comfort.

Everything seems different after cry.

Clear tears, healing agents of our soul.

그림은 손으로 그리는 것이지만,

결코, 손으로만 그리는 것이 아니다.

내 마음속의 모든 사고와 내 삶의 방식까지,

그 모든 것이 그림으로 표현되어 나오는 것이다.

그래서 그림은 정직하다.

—

Painting is drawn by hands.

However, it is not just drawn by hands.

From all the thoughts in my mind to all my ways of life

All of them are expressed in my paintings.

So, the paintings are honest.

16 | Old Story 162 x 130cm Mixed media on canvas. 1998

17

캄캄한 어둠 속에서 물끄러미 그림을 보다 보면,
어렴풋이 그림이 보이기 시작한다.
이른 새벽이나 늦은 밤,
나는 불을 끄고 물끄러미 그림을 바라보곤 한다.
그러다 보면, 그림이 나에게 말을 걸어온다.
밝을 때 보는 그림의 느낌과 무척이나 다르지만,
왠지 더 진실된 느낌을 받는 듯한…

—

In the black darkness of the darkness,
when I stare at the paintings blankly,
The paintings begin to blur faintly.
At early dawn or late night,
I turn off the lights and stare at the paintings blankly.
Then, the paintings come to talk to me.
It is totally different from the feeling of the paintings
I see on bright days.
Somehow, it seems to be getting more trueful…

17 | Untitled 182 x 123cm Mixed media on canvas. 2000

Untitled 194 x 260cm Mixed media on canvas, 1999

여러 번 시행착오를 거쳐서
건져 올린 자연스러운 드로잉과 오브제.
오랜 시간과 땀의 흔적들이 고스란히
화면의 배경이 된다.

—

After many trials and errors,
the natural drawings and objects are brought out.
Long time and sign of sweat
become the background of the paintings.

19 | Untitled 163 x 130cm Mixed media on canvas. 1999

끊임없이 부딪힌다.

마찰이 일어난다. 불꽃이 튄다.

그 불꽃 속에서야 비로소 새로운 탄생이 일어난다.

용광로 속에서 녹아가며 끊임없이 변해 가듯이.

작업이란 때로는 서로 부딪히고 싸워가며

그 속에서 새로운 질서를 찾아내는 것이다.

우리는 삶이란 용광로 안에서 하루하루 끝없이 부딪혀 내는 것이다.

우리는 하루하루 새로이 탄생되어진다.

—

Constant conflict.

Friction occurs. The sparks fly up.

It is only in the flame where new birth takes place.

Like melting in furnace and changing constantly,

creating works is a battle

to find new order in it through conflicts and fights.

We live in an endless bombardment of the day in furnace.

We are reborn every day.

20 | Untitled 163 x 130cm Mixed media on canvas. 1999

바람에 어질러져 있는 물감 자국들.

세월이 지나가며 남긴 흔적이 고스란히 바닥에 남아 있다.

내 삶의 소중한 일부분이 이곳에서 이루어졌다.

고맙다, 이 모든 것이…

—

The paint marks messing with the wind

The trace of left-overs still remains on the floor.

Precious part of my life was realized here.

Thank you, all this…

21 | Untitled 194 x 260cm Mixed media on canvas. 1999

흰색!

가장 완전하게 아름다운 색.

나는 이렇게 표현하고 싶다.

색에는 여러 가지 감정이 있다.

그냥 바라보고만 있어도 마음이 맑아지는 색도 있다.

무한한 가능성의 색.

그러나 가장 위험한 색이 흰색이다.

—

White!

Most completely beautiful color.

I would like to express it with it.

Colors have many different emotions.

Some colors that make my mind clear just by their looks.

Colors of infinite possibilities.

However, white is the most dangerous.

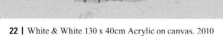

22 | White & White 130 x 40cm Acrylic on canvas. 2010

22

그림은 참 마음대로 그려지지 않는다.

난 이것을 원했는데 나의 손은 이미

다른 방향으로 달아날 때도 있다.

모든 것이 마음대로 잘되지 않을 때가 많다.

이런 날, 난 바흐를 들으며

묵직한 첼로의 선율만을 느낄 때가 있다.

—

Painting is not easy to draw as we wish.

When I want it this way, my hands run away in different way.

There are many times when everything can not be done at my will.

On such day, I listen to Bach.

There are times when I hear only the melody of

a low-tone ponderous cello.

원재료가 가진 거친 맛

우린 어쩌면 세련된 것에 길들여 졌는지 모르겠지만

오랜 장맛의 느낌처럼 세월의 힘을 견딘,

혀끝의 달콤함이 아닌 온몸의 전율로 기억되는 맛

그런 기억이 되고 싶다.

나의 그림은.

—

Rough taste of raw materials

We might be tamed by the sophisticated things.

Like a feeling of long-lasting taste of fermented paste,

not the sweetness of the tip of the tongue

but the taste that is memorized by the whole body's thrill.

I want to make such taste memory.

With my paintings.

23 | Untitled 163 x 130cm Mixed media on canvas. 2006

하얀 캔버스 천 위에

최소한 여덟 번이나 아홉 번의 반복 과정을 거치면서

마티에르가 생기고 하나의 화면이 된다.

그래서 작업은 새로운 질서를 찾아가는 과정이다.

서로 다른 물질들이 모여서

하나의 호흡으로 마무리되는…

—

On white canvas cloth

over at least eight or nine repeated processes

Martière comes up to realize one image.

So, work can be called a process of finding new order.

Different substances gather together

It is finished with one breath…

25 | Untitled 164 x 130cm Mixed media on canvas. 2006

작업은 끊임없는 반복과 지우기로 행해진다.

지우고, 다시 그리고.

다시 그리고, 또다시 지우고.

그 겹쳐지는 시간 속에 우리의 삶이 있다.

중요한 것으로 여겼던 가치들이 시간이 흐르면서

차츰차츰 빛을 잃어가기도 하고,

하잘것없다고 여겼던 것들이 빛을 발하기도 한다.

저 노랑을 보라. 묵묵히 모든 것을 받아들이고 있다.

잔잔한 슬픔도.

언뜻언뜻 배어 나오는 희망의 꽃들도.

—

A work is realized with constant repetitions and erasures.

Erase and then erase one more time.

Again and again. Erase again.

Our lives exist and last in such overlapping time.

Over time, the values that we considered important

gradually lose their light.

Things that I thought were very trivial sometimes shine.

Look at the yellow. It silently accepts everything without a word.

Still sadness.

The hopeful flowers which suddenly raise their heads up here and there.

PART 2

"순수한 색채·맑고 깨끗한 회화"

"Pure color, clear and clean painting."

예술을 통한 영혼의 치유, 긍정을 추구하는 서정자의 작품세계

Healing the Spirit Through Art, Jeong-Ja Seo Pursues Positivity Through Paint

서정자는 그리스 드라마를 통한 영적 정화 감지를 설명한 아리스토텔레스의 경험과 삶의 근본적인 고통에서 벗어나기 위한 예술의 필요성을 주장하는 니체의 투쟁, 예술이 억압된 성적 충동에 의해 유발된 불안을 완화하는데 도움이 된다는 프로이트의 가설을 작품에 인용한다. 이러한 각기 다른 철학들이 그녀의 캔버스 안에서 어떻게 어우러지는지는 바로 그녀의 유능한 컬러 배색 사용을 통해 여실히 드러난다.

의미를 내포하고 있는 모호한 레이어들의 짙은 색 사각형을 활용한 마크 로스코와 같이 서정자의 작업 구성은 주로 사각형 속에 다른 사각형을 배치하는 식으로 한정한다. 이 같은 단순한 형태 요소는 그녀의 색감에 더욱 활기를 불어 넣어주고 돋보이게 하는 역할을 한다. 짙은 보라색과 영묘한 청색, 마치 타는 듯한 붉은 색감들은 그녀의 캔버스로부터 피어오른다. 그녀는 관객들에게 우리를 정의하는 톤을 내포하는 시각과 감정의 의미에 대한 경험으로 초대하는 한편, 자연에 대한 시상이나 우리를 둘러싸고 있는 세계의 환영을 지워 버리기도 한다. 그녀의 색, 즉 서정자의 의식이 의미하려 하는 것은 전체적으로는 조용하고 온화하지만 불안감으로부터 완전히 자유롭지는 않다. 그녀의 작품을 보면, 색의 가장자리에서 오는 어떤 긴장감은 그림에 활력을 준다. 전반적으로, 서정자는 색에 정화와 치유의 힘이 있다고 믿고 있다. 그녀의 작품의 전반에 걸친 색상들은 스스로 변형되는데 - 레드가 옐로로, 녹색은 블랙에 가까울 정도로 아주 어두워지거나 연녹색과 같이 화사해지기도 한다. 하지만 그 역동성은 일정하다. 그녀의 작품 대다수는 흥미롭고 즐거운 감성을 보여준다.

Jeong-Ja Seo cites the experiences of Aristotle who described sensing spiritual purification through Greek drama, Nietzsche's contention that art is needed to escape life's fundamental pain, and Freud's hypothesis that art helps alleviate anxiety induced by repressed sexual urges. How these disparate thoughts come into play on her canvases is largely orchestrated through her use of color.

As Mark Rothko utilized squares of dense color that obscure layers of work while enabling layers of meaning, Jeong-Ja Seo confines her compositional elements predominantly to squares within squares. Her simplicity of form supports and benefits the vibrancy of her colors. Dense purples, ethereal blues and searing reds burst forth from her canvases. She invites viewers to experience the sense of sight and the emotion inherent in the tones that define our world, but removes any precise reference to nature or the world around us.

Jeong-Ja Seo states that her colors are meant to be, on the whole, calm and placid, but not entirely free from anxiety. The hint of tension at the edges of color creates a feeling of energy in her work. Overall, she believes that color has the power to both cleanse and heal. Throughout the body of her work, the colors themselves change – red replaces yellow, green may be so dark as to border on black or be as bright as spring grass – but the vibrancy is constant. Many of her paintings suggest a playful, joyful sensibility.

메리 그레고리
Mary Gregory

Mary Gregory는 미술 평론가이자 작가, 소설가이다. 그녀의 글은 뉴욕의 유망한 잡지들과 신문에 자주 소개된다. 그녀는 뉴욕에서 괄목 받은 전시들과 작가들을 리뷰하고 인터뷰한다. Mary Gregory 는 2015년에 New York Press, Association for Best Coverage of the Arts 팀에 소속되어 있었으며 2012, 2014, 그리고 2015년에는 Pushcart Prize 수상후보자로 지목되었다.

Mary Gregory is an award-winning art critic, writer, and novelist. Her articles appear regularly in some of the leading magazines and newspapers in New York. She has reviewed landmark exhibitions and interviewed and written features on top figures in the New York art world. Mary Gregory is part of a team honored by the New York Press Association for Best Coverage of the Arts in 2015, and she is a 2013, 2014 and 2015 Pushcart Prize nominee.

26 | Saekdong 489 x 130cm Acrylic on canvas. 2010

26

수많은 색들이 춤을 춘다.

서로 뒤엉켜서 춤을 춘다.

초록이 빨강을 초대한다.

빨강은 새로이 노랑과 친구가 된다.

점이 모여서, 선이 되고, 선이 모여서 커다란 춤이 만들어진다.

우리는 하나의 우주, 그 위에 작은 점들로 연결되어 있고,

그 점들은 또다시 선으로 연결되어 있다.

너, 그리고 나, 우리.

그래서 혼자는 살아갈 수 없다.

함께 부족함을 채워 나가야만 한다.

함께 어울리자, 함께 춤을 추자.

모든 것을 내어줄 수 있을 때 진정한 우리가 된다.

보상 없는 마음.

그것이 우리를 더 넓고 커다란 그릇으로 만든다.

—

Multiple colors are dancing.

They dance all tangled up together.

Green invites red.

Red becomes a new friend of yellow.

Dots are gathered to make a line

and the lines are gathered to make a big dance.

We are connected by single universe with small dots on it.

The dots are connected by a line again.

You and I, We

Therefore, we can't live alone.

Together, we should fill the gap.

Let's mingle together. Let's dance together.

When we can give everything away, we can be true 'We'.

Compensation-less Mind

It make us better person with greater potential.

27 | Healing 194 x 130cm Acrylic on canvas. 2012

파랑의 공간, 빨강의 공간, 초록의 공간.

나의 공간, 너의 공간, 우리의 공간.

공간을 겹쳐서 표현하다 보면, 그만 아득해질 때가 있다.

저 심연 너머에 무언가가 잡힐 듯…

초록을 겹쳐가며 점점 더 깊은 울림을 표현하고 싶었다.

우리의 작은 숨구멍으로, 작은 손 떨림으로…

우리는 우리 삶의 주인공이다.

—

Blue Space, red space, green space.

My space, your space, our space.

There is time when I express them by overlapping space.

Maybe, we can catch some meanings beyond their abyss…

I wanted to express more deep echoes by overlapping green colors.

With our little pores, with small hand trembling…

We, ourselves are the protagonists of our lives.

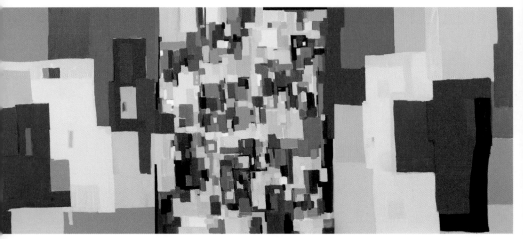

28 | Saekdong 489 x 130cm Acrylic on canvas. 2010

28

꽃은 끊임없이 애쓴다.

메마른 아스팔트 위에 뿌리를 내리고,

조금 더 손을 뻗어 햇살을 어루만진다.

그렇기에 꽃은 아름답다.

이름 하나 모르고 무심하게 피어 있지만,

그 자체로 아름다운 것이다.

무심한 아름다움,

그림 또한 무심한 아름다움이 있어야만 한다고 생각한다.

자신의 자리에서 오랫동안 뻗어 나가는 저 이름 모를 꽃처럼.

비록 자신의 이름 하나 없더라도…

—

Flowers constantly try.

Rooting down into dry asphalt,

they try to reach out their hands further to touch the sunshine.

So, the flowers are beautiful.

They bloom blankly without knowing any name.

They are beautiful as themselves.

Blank beauty

I think that paintings should also have blank beauty.

Like the flowers that stretch for a long time in their places

without any name, even if you do not have your own name...

29 | 01:30am at Hyderabad Airport 100 x 100cm Mixed media on canvas. 2016

오래되고 낡은,

그러나 소중한 붓 한 자루.

오래전 베이징에서 샀던 닭털로 만들어진 붓 한 자루.

나와 함께해 온 세월이 10여 년이 넘어간다.

닳아 버려서 뭉툭해진 낡은 붓이 정겹다.

—

Old, worn

but one precious piece of brush.

A brush made of chicken hairs that I bought in Beijing long ago.

The years that the brush has been with me are over ten years.

The old brush and I, we are so affectionate.

그림은 색채 사이의 미묘한 관계를 구축하는 것이다.
나아가고 물러나고 확장하고 축소되면서
자유로운 융합과 정서를 통해
미적 체험을 느낄 수 있도록 하는 것.
우리의 삶에 기쁨과 위로를 건네는 것.

—

The painting is to build subtle relationship among colors.
Moving on, retreating, expanding, and shrinking,
through free convergence and sharing emotions
it is something to make us have aesthetic experience.
It is something to pass joy and comfort down to our lives.

30 | Saekdong 326 x 130cm Acrylic on canvas. 2010

31 | 01:30am at Hyderabad Airport 91 x 73cm Acrylic on canvas. 2016

31

나는 후각에 민감하다.

낯선 도시에 가면

그 도시의 냄새가 바람에 실려 온다.

열대과일 향처럼 달콤한 도시가 있고,

다소 불쾌하고…

간혹 지저분한 냄새가 나는 도시도 있다.

그러나 달콤함과 불쾌감이 섞일 때는

굉장히 섹시한 냄새가 난다.

어쩌면 불행 속에 따뜻한 희망이 숨어 있는 것처럼…

절묘한 섞임.

—

I have a sensitive sense of smell.

When I go to a strange city,

I can feel the smell of the city comes from the wind.

Some cities are sweet like the tropical fruit flavor.

Some cities have dirty smell which is somewhat uncomfortable...

But when sweetness and discomfort are mixed

I can feel the sexy smell.

It seems like warm is hidden by the unhappiness...

Exquisite mixing.

인도 전통 안료를 섞어서

드로잉을 했다.

꽃을 그린 것이 아니었는데

꽃처럼 보였다.

우연히 나타난 형상

그래서 멈춰버렸다. 그림을…

어쩌면 카르마.

—

I painted with mixing traditional Indian pigments.

It didn't mean flowers.

But they looked like flowers

Accidentally appearing shapes,

so I stopped. The paintings…

Maybe, It's karma.

33 | White & White 91 x 117cm Acrylic on canvas. 2006

새로움은 문을 열고 나왔을 때 생긴다.

낯섦을 통해서 더 큰 확장으로.

새로운 뭔가를 원한다면

낡은 생각을 던져 버리고

길을 나서자.

창조는 변방에 있다.

—

Newness occurs when you open the door.

With greater expansion through strangeness.

if you want something new,

throw out old ideas

Take the road.

Creation is on the fringe.

그저 소리 없이 하루하루.

이 공간의 공기들과 내 작업실 속 사물들과

도란도란 이야기할 때가 있다.

내 곁에 있어 줘서 고마워.

낡은 연필과 닳아버린 붓…

—

Just one day after another day with no sound.

There is a time that I talk to the air in this space

and the objects in my studio.

Thanks for staying with me.

My old pencil and worn brush…

34 | Untitled 91 x 117cm Acrylic on canvas. 2006

작업에서의 결합과 융합.

나는 지금 그 새로움을 갈망하고 있다.

함께 섞어보는 것,

재미있는 생각이 떠올랐다.

적어보고 실험해 보고 해부해 보자.

그냥, 그냥 해보자.

—

Combination and fusion created in my art work.

I crave for that newness now.

To mix them together

Interesting thoughts came up to my mind.

Let's try to write down, experiment, and dissect.

Just, let's just try.

35 | Untitled 40 x 40cm Mixed media on canvas. 2006

36 | Healing 73 x 50cm Acrylic on canvas. 2015

나의 작업은 어쩌면 단순하다고 생각할 수도 있다.

그러나 단순함은 시간을 끌지 않는다.

바로 본론이기 때문에 집중할 수 있다.

그저 색이 가지고 있는 공간감에 집중하기 때문이다.

—

My work is seemed to be simple.

But simplicity does not take time to understand.

You can catch it right away because it is just a main point.

It just focuses on the sense of space that color has.

37 | Healing 73 x 61cm Acrylic on canvas. 2015

37
—

오후에 마시는 커피 한잔.
마음처럼 그림이 잘되지 않는 날.
그냥 말없이, 따뜻한 커피 한잔만으로
마음의 위로를 받고는 한다.
또다시 해보자.

—

A cup of coffee in the afternoon.
The day when the painting doesn't follow my mind.
I am comforted for my heart
with a warm cup of coffee, silently.
Let's try it again.

38 | 01:30am at Hyderabad Airport 73 x 61cm Mixed media on canvas. 2016

38

따뜻한 노랑

차가운 노랑

밝은 노랑

약간 흐린 노랑

진한 노랑

무척이나 많은 노랑을 표현할 수 있다.

그러나 보통 사람들은 한 가지 노랑만 기억하고는 한다.

—

Warm yellow

Cool yellow

Bright yellow

Slightly light yellow

Deep yellow

A little light yellow

I can express so many yellows.

But only one yellow remains in ordinary people's memories.

39 | Healing 162 x 130cm Acrylic on canvas. 2015

어쩌면 우리의 삶은 마치,

저 창문 너머 보이는 푸른 숲처럼 한 가지 색이 아니겠지요.

때로는 비바람 불고 폭풍이 몰아치겠지만,

따뜻한 봄날 노란색 태양이 우리 곁에 있는 것처럼.

—

Maybe, our lives are like,

They might not be one color like the green forests that we can see

beyond that window.

It may sometimes rain and storm but

as the yellow sun is beside us on a warm spring day.

마찰을 통한 새로운 발견.

작업도 때로는 서로 부딪히고 싸우며

그 속에서 질서를 찾아가는 것이다.

우리가 하루하루 부딪히면서 새로운 탄생을 하는 것처럼.

—

New discovery through friction.

Works sometimes conflict and fight

They seek order from them.

Just as we bump into one another and make new birth.

40 | Healing 227 x 162cm Acrylic on canvas. 2015

41 | Healing 73 x 91cm Acrylic on canvas. 2015

가장 정직한 도형, 사각형.

한 번 두 번 붓질로 본질을 그려보고 싶었다.

삶의 본질.

어쩌면 우리 모두는 그 사각형 속에 갇혀 있는 것이고,

또한 열려 있는 것이다.

—

The most honest shape, rectangle.

I wanted to draw the essence with brush strokes once or twice.

The essence of life.

Maybe, we are all trapped in the square.

Maybe, we are also open.

42 | Untitled 73 x 61cm Mixed media on canvas, 2004

무엇이든 담아낸다.

그 시간, 그 공간, 그 순간,

그대로 그림은 멈춰 있지만

동시에 누구보다도 역동적으로 움직인다.

끊임없이 흐르는 생기 있는 피로써,

끝없이 성장해 가는 영혼으로써.

—

It carries whatever in it.

The time, the space, and the moment,

The painting stays still there without moves.

At the same time, they move more dynamically than anyone else.

With constantly flowing blood

and with soul growing eternally.

01:30 Am at Hyderabad Airport.

내가 처음 인도를 접한 곳이다.

청회색의 달콤한 바람과 마주한 곳.

나의 이번 작품에 내재시킨 가치들은,

시간을 함축하고 싶었던 것이다.

사원의 오래된 벽으로부터, 흙바람, 돌…

오래된 시간의 의미.

—

01:30 AM at Hyderabad Airport.

It is where I first encountered India.

It is the place where I face the sweet wind of blue-gray color.

The values kept in my works

I wanted to imply and implicate time in them.

From the old walls of the temple, dirt, stone…

Meaning of old time.

43 | 01:30am at Hyderabad Airport 73 x 61cm Acrylic on canvas. 2016

44 | Untitled 91 x 73cm Mixed media on canvas. 2004

들어온다.

봄을 닮은 노란색, 끝없이 불타오르는 빨간색,

오랜 친구처럼 무심한 듯 정겨운 하늘색까지.

마음속으로 쏟아져 들어온다.

빠르게, 빠르면서도 부드럽게.

왜 이리 늦었냐고, 왜 이제 오느냐고 채근 댄다.

어린아이처럼 밝다, 즐거움이 피어오른다.

—

Coming in.

Yellow resembling spring, endless burning red,

and adorable and indifferent sky blue like my old friends.

pour into my mind.

Fast, fast but smooth.

they urge, asking why you are so late and coming now.

Bright like young children and pleasures bloom.

45
—

복잡한 일들과 복잡한 관계.
온통 복잡한 것투성이 사이에서
오늘도 어김없이 해가 저문다.
복잡한 일들을 마무리하고,
복잡한 복도를 지나 집으로 향한다.
오늘도 어김없이 하루가 저문다.

—

Complex things and relationships.
Among all the complex things,
the sun still sets today.
Finishing complicated things,
I head for home through complex hallways.
Today, the sun definitely sets down.

46 | Untitled 194 x 260cm Mixed media on canvas. 1999

그림 속에 광활한 자연을 담을 수는 없을까.
그래서 나무를 그리는 대신 온통 초록색으로
내 마음속의 자연을 덮어 버렸다.
그 숲의 바람이 나에게 손짓한다.
내 안으로 들어오라고.

—

Can I have vast nature in my painting?
So, instead of drawing trees with all green
I covered my canvas with the nature in my mind.
The wind from the forest beckons me,
inviting me to come in.

우리 삶은 완벽하지만은 않아서,

때로는 겉으로 삐뚤빼뚤한 태가 나기도 한다.

또 겉만 보고 자신의 색을 부정하기도 한다.

하지만 걱정하지 마라.

마음속에 칠해진 당신만의 색이 곧 당신이다.

조금은 서투른 당신이,

남들과는 다른 당신이.

—

Since our lives are not perfect,

they sometimes twisted seemingly.

In addition, they also deny their colors by looking at their surface.

But do not worry.

You are the color of your own painted in your mind.

A little clumsy but

you are different from others.

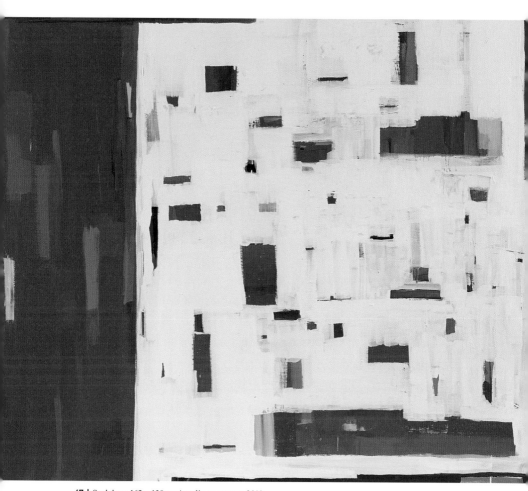

47 | Saekdong 162 x 130cm Acrylic on canvas. 2010

우리 사회는 항상 정도正道만 강요해서,

못난 것이나 모난 것을 허용하지 않는다.

좀 모났으면 어떠한가, 못났으면 어떠한가.

정도가 모여서 모난 우리가 되는 것인데.

—

Our society is always forced to do correct ways.

It does not allow anything bad or perfect.

What matters if it is a little bit lonely or sometimes go bad?

At the end, such correct ways come to realize imperfect us.

48 | Saekdong 100 x 100cm Acrylic on canvas. 2010

49 | Healing 91 x 73cm Acrylic on canvas. 2015

세상에는 다양한 문이 존재한다.

많은 사람들은

견고하고 튼튼한 문을 원한다.

그러나 어쩌면 그 문은 단절이 될 수 있다.

햇살도 들어오고 바람도 쉴 수 있는

문을…

—

Various doors exist in the world.

Many people

they want solid and sturdy doors.

But maybe that door can be a disconnect.

Through which the sun is coming in and the wind can rest

the doors…

50 | Saekdong 163 x 130cm Acrylic on canvas. 2010

처음에는 색동의 화려함을 표현하고 싶었다.

또, 눈처럼 맑디맑은 어린아이의 웃음도 표현해 내고 싶었다.

그러나 밝음 속에 잔잔하게 슬픔이 배어 나왔다.

그림을 그린다는 것은 어쩌면, 슬픔을 녹여내는 것일지도 모른다.

말간 슬픔으로, 맑은 눈물로 다시 한 번 태어나는 것이다.

나는 그래서 그림이 좋다.

말간 슬픔으로 다시 태어나, 슬픔을 녹여내는 힘…

—

At first, I wanted to express the splendor of coloring.

I also wanted to express the smile of a child who was as clear as snow.

But from the brightness, calm sadness grew.

Drawing paintings may be a meltdown of sadness.

It is to be born once again with clear sorrow and tears.

That's why I like painting.

Power to dissolve sadness, reborn with clear sadness…

51 | Untitled 230 x 182cm Mixed media on canvas. 2001

작업을 하다 보면 문제에 부딪힐 때가 많다.

그러나 나는 답에 집중한다.

답을 먼저 생각하면 답이 떠오르지만,

문제를 먼저 생각하면 문제만 생각난다.

그리고 다양성을 통해 해결 방법을 생각한다.

사물이 극에 달하면 반드시 역전되는 것처럼.

목표도 마찬가지이다.

먼저, 정하고 방법을 찾아가는 것이다.

미친 듯이 달려서 임계점을 향해 가는 것

나는 그것을 열정이라고 믿는다.

—

There are a lot of problems I face while painting.

But I would rather focus on the answers.

If I think of the answers first, the answers pop up to my head.

But if I think of the problems first, I just stick to the problems.

And I think of the solutions through diversity.

As things reach the pole, they seem to be reversed.

The goals are same.

First of all, I decide the goals first

and try to find the ways to reach them.

Running crazy and heading for critical points

I believe this act to find answers, a passion.

52 | Healing 162 x 130cm Acrylic on canvas. 2015

오늘도 어김없이 작업실에 출근한다.

외투를 벗고는 차를 한잔 우린다.

첫 느낌이

달다.

우두커니, 어제 그린 그림들을

보며 짧은 시간 상념에 잠겨 든다.

—

I go to my studio today as usual.

I take off my coat and brew a cup of tea.

First feeling,

It is sweet.

Blankly, I look at the paintings that I drew yesterday

I lost in a conception for a while.

53 | Untitled 61 x 73cm Mixed media on canvas. 2004

봄에 퍼지는 햇살의 느낌과 여름에 퍼지는 햇살의 느낌은 다르다.

그래서 우리의 모든 것은 시간과 공간의 의미가 크다고 생각한다.

그 시각, 그 장소.

때로는 잊지 못할 의미가 될 수 있다.

갑자기 바다가 생각나는 아침이다.

그 푸른 물빛 드리워진 내 젊음의 영혼…

—

The feeling of sunshine spreading in the spring

and the feeling of sunshine spreading in the summer are different.

So, I think that all of us have meaningful time and space.

That time, that place.

Sometimes, it can mean something unforgettable.

Suddenly, it is the morning, reminding me of the sea.

My young soul draped by the blue water light…

시간은 영원성을 내포하지 않는다.

그 속의 빛의 흐름, 흐름의 속도.

화면을 채우는 시간, 공간의 의미…

그러므로 난 매일 새롭다.

날마다 새로운 그림을, 새로움을 그려낼 것이다.

그 새로움은 결국 쌓이고 쌓여 세월이 되어 갈 것이다.

—

Time does not imply eternity.

The flow of light in it and the speed of flow.

Time to fill the picture, meaning of space…

Therefore, I am new every day.

I will draw new paintings and fresh things every day.

The newness will be eventually accumulated on and on

to become years.

54 | Saekdong 100 x 100cm Mixed media on canvas. 2014

아무것도 정해진 것은 없다.

그저 순간과 순간, 한 흔적, 그리고 한 흔적.

언제나 그렇게 그려가는 것일 뿐.

그렇기에 나는,

나는 그림에 의미를 부여하고 싶지 않다.

—

Nothing is determined.

Just moments and moments, a track of trace, and a trail.

It is always drawn like that.

Therefore,

I do not want to give meaning to the painting.

55 | Untitled 61 x 73cm Mixed media on canvas. 2004

56 | Healing 91 x 73cm Acrylic on canvas. 2015

56
—

마음에 햇볕이 필요하다.

지금,

나는…

—

I need the sunshine of my heart.

57 | Healing 97 x 163cm Acrylic on canvas. 2012

57

우리의 삶은 인문학적 훈련을 통해

성장한다고 생각한다.

인문학적 훈련이란 예술과 함께

통찰력 그리고 상상력

끊임없이 그 두 가지를 연결해 나가는 것이다.

그림을 직접 보고, 새로움을 떠올리며,

좋은 음악을 듣고…

그러다 보면 몸이 체득을 해나가고,

그것이 쌓여서 새로움이 탄생하는 것이다.

책을 미친 듯이 읽어야 하는 이유이고,

또한 미친 듯이 그려야 하는 이유이다.

—

I think our lives grow through

trainings of humanities.

Trainings of humanities mean to connect insight

and imagination constantly with art.

Looking at painting, thinking of new things,

listening to good music...

If so, your body will learn,

what you learn will be accumulates

and newness will be born.

That's the reason I need to read books crazily.

Also, that's the reason I need to draw crazily.

58 | Healing 73 x 61cm Acrylic on canvas. 2015

단순함은 곧 본론이다.

애써 시간을 들일 필요가 없다.

곧장 들어가 중요한 것에만 집중할 수 있다.

때로 그림이 단순하다는 것은

무서우리만큼 겁이 날 때가 있다.

즉, 본질을 말하는 것이다.

위선과 가식을 뺀, 본질 그 자체.

—

Simplicity is main point itself.

You do not have to spend hours trying.

You can jump to it directly and concentrate only on what are important.

Sometimes, the fact that painting is simple

makes me afraid and terrified.

It is because it tells essentials.

That is to say, the essence.

Essence itself without hypocrisy and pretense.

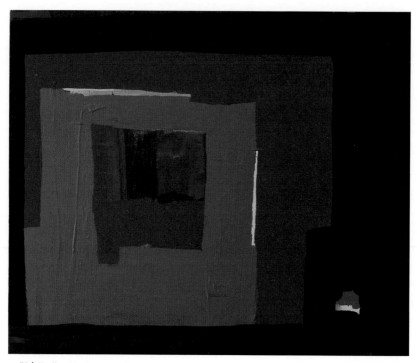

59 | Healing 73 x 61cm Acrylic on canvas. 2012

"나 스스로가 먼저 세상에 일어날 그 변화가 되어야 한다."

간디의 이 한마디를 가슴 깊숙이 새겨두자.

미래를 객관적으로, 나를 객관적으로 바라볼 수 있어야 한다.

스스로가 세상의 변화가 되어야 한다.

쉽지 않다는 걸 안다.

왜냐하면, 지금의 내 모습에 너무나도 익숙해져 있기 때문이다.

나의 내면부터 잔잔한 변화를 일으키자.

그 내면의 고요한 변화를 성장시켜, 세상의 변화를 만들자.

—

"I must be the change that will happen to the world first."

Let's put this word of Gandhi deep in our minds.

We should be able to look at the future objectively and me, too.

We must be able to be a change of the world.

I know it is not easy.

Because we am so accustomed to what we are now.

Let's make calm change from my inside.

Let's make the world change by growing calm inner change.

60

1/1000.

시장을 지배하는 대단한 물건.

역사적으로 보면 그 물건은 고작 1/1000이라고 한다.

그렇다면 작가로 성공할 확률은?

그런 생각일랑 접어두자.

그냥 묵묵하게 나의 길을 걸어나가자.

성공이 대단한 것인가?

단지, 지금 이 순간 그림을 그려나갈 수 있어서 행복한 것이다.

그래서 나는, 나는 이미 성공한 작가이다.

—

1/1000.

A great object that dominates the market.

Historically, such object is just 1/1000.

Then, what is the probability of being a successful writer?

Let's break such thought.

Let's just walk our ways silently.

Is success something great?

I am just happy to be able to draw my painting at

this moment right now.

So I am, I am an already successful artist.

61 | Healing 100 x 100cm Acrylic on canvas. 2015

우리의 사유 과정이란,
우리가 본 것을 우리가 알고 있는 것과
연관시킬 때 비로소 시작된다.
하지만 그 과정에서 창의력이 없다면,
그 사유는 살아 있는 것일까, 죽어 있는 것일까?
창의력은 문제 해결 능력이다.
뒤집어서 생각해 보자.
발견해 내어 보자.
다르게 생각하는 것.
우리의 사유 과정이란,
우리가 본 것을 뒤집어 보고, 발견해 내는 것이다.
전과는 다르게 생각해 내는 것이다.

—

Our process of thinking,
it begins only when we can associate
what we have seen with what we know.
But if you do not have creativity in the process,
is that reason alive or dead?
Creativity is problem solving ability.
Let's think over.
Let's try to find out.
Thinking differently.
The process of our thinking
is to overturn and discover what we have seen.
It is to think out differently unlike before.

하얗고 네모난 캔버스는,

세상과 닮은 점이 많다.

끊임없이 계속되는 창조 속에서,

비로소 새로움이 탄생한다.

그 새로움들이 모여서 조화를 이루고,

그 조화는 아름답다.

그래서 그림 속에는 우주가 있다.

그림 속에서는 우주를 발견하는 기쁨이 있다.

—

The white and square canvas,

it has many things that resemble the world.

In the constant creation,

finally, newness is born.

The new are gathered to make harmony.

The harmony is beautiful.

So, we can find universe in the paintings.

It is a great joy to discover the universe in the paintings.

62 | Saekdong 40 x 50cm Mixed media on canvas. 2010

63 | Saekdong 163 x 130cm Mixed media on canvas. 2010

"나는 작품을 구매하는 어떤 사람도 시험할 수가 없다.

내 작품을 소유한 사람은, 누구든 나를 소유한 것이다.

내 마음을 소유한 것이나 다름이 없다."

어느 작가의 이 말처럼,

내 작품은 내 마음이다.

세상의 단 하나의 작품,

그래서 나의 인생을 갖는 것이다.

—

"I can not test anyone who purchases my works.

Anyone who owns my works is like someone who owns me.

It is like owning my mind."

As one artist says,

my works are shape of my mind.

The only work in the world

So, purchasing it is like owning my life.

64 | 01:30am at Hyderabad Airport 100 x 100cm Acrylic on canvas. 2016

물감을 섞어서 색을 만들다 보면,

가끔씩 미친 듯이 좋은 색이 나온다.

약간의 결핍도 가끔씩 좋은 작품으로 이어지기도 한다.

완벽한 색이 있을까?

과연 완벽한 색으로 그리면 완벽한 작품이 나올까?

나는 의문을 가져본다.

2% 부족한 언어가 바로 그림이다.

—

When I make colors by mixing paints,

Sometimes I get amazing colors.

Some deficiencies sometimes lead to good works.

Is there any perfect color?

If you paint with perfect colors,

do you think you can make perfect works?

I have a question.

The language of 2% deficiency is painting.

잘 기억나지는 않지만,

글을 쓴다는 것은 내 몸이라는 실을 풀어서

새로운 옷을 짜는 과정이라고 했다…

작업, 그림 또한 내 몸의 실을 풀어서 새로움을 짜는 것이다.

낡은 생각과 사고들을 따뜻함을 담아

새로이 담아내는 과정인 것이다.

씨실과 날실의 교차,

그 속에서 또 다른 무엇인가가 꿈틀대며 올라오는 것.

—

I am not sure but it said,

"Writing is untangling strings of my body and weaving new clothes"

Works and painting also unfolds thread of my body to create the new.

Warmth of old thoughts and thoughts

it is a new process to keep them in fresh way.

The intersection of weft and warp,

something new comes up from it, giving wiggles.

65 | Healing 100 x 100cm Acrylic on canvas. 2012

66 | Untitled 91 x 117cm Mixed media on canvas. 2002

작업실에 난로 하나가 고장이 났다.

싸늘하다 못해서, 춥고 손이 시리지만 정신이 번쩍 든다.

나는 지금 무엇을 하고 있나?

왜?

왜 그림을 그리는 것일까?

그 물음이 나의 가슴을 파고든다.

겨울… 정신 차리자.

—

One of the stoves in my workplace is broken.

It is cold and freezing. My hands are cold.

But I have much sobering thought.

What am I doing now?

Why?

Why do I draw paintings?

That question digs into my heart.

Winter… I need to throw myself into my work.

67 | Untitled 61 x 73cm Mixed media on canvas. 2002

67

열려 있는 그림을 그리고 싶다.

누구든지 빼꼼 하고 들어와 쉴 수 있는.

그리하여 가슴이 답답해서 미칠 듯한 사랑에 실컷 울 수 있는.

행복의 절정을 맛보고 있는 사람은 행복을 오래도록 느낄 수 있는…

그런 그림을 그리고 싶다.

사유하고, 쉴 수 있고,

함께 가슴을 내줄 수 있는 그림.

그런 그림을 그리고 싶다.

누군가에게는 위로가,

누군가에게는 사랑이,

누군가에게는 희망이.

누군가에게는 기댈 수 있는 나무가 되고 싶다.

—

I want to draw open paintings

where anyone can come in and take a rest

where I can cry in crazy love with oppressed mind

where a person who tastes the pinnacle of happiness can feel the

happiness for a long time.

I want to draw such paintings

where I can think and rest together

where I can share my opinion together.

I want to draw such paintings.

Comfort for someone,

Love for someone,

Hope for someone.

I want to be a tree that someone can lean on.

68 | 01:30am at Hyderabad Airport 61 x 73cm Acrylic on canvas. 2016

나의 삶을 탐구하고 꿈을 꾸려면 무엇부터 해야 할까?

그냥 떠나보는 것이다. 아무런 생각도 하지 말고, 새로움을 향해서.

골목길이든, 진흙탕이든, 비바람이 불고 천둥이 쳐도.

용감하게 맨몸으로 부딪혀 보는 것이다.

그렇게 경험이 쌓이면 좀 더 멀리 갈 수 있을 것이다.

작업도 마찬가지이다. 머리를 믿고 들어가 보면 한 가지는 건진다.

아… 아직 멀었구나.

그러나 기다려라, 내가 간다.

What should I do to explore my life and dream?

I just need to try to leave. Towards newness without any thinking

Whether it is alleyway or mud, windy, or stormy.

I bravely need to bump with my body.

With such accumulated experiences, you can go further.

Work is the same. When you trust and start it,

you will get at least one thing.

Ah… It's still far away to go.

But wait, I must go.

버리고, 선택하고, 집중하는 것은 그림에도 필요하다.

무엇을 버릴 것인지, 그리고 무엇에 집중해야 하는지.

그리고 무엇을 선택해야 하는지.

그것들은 오로지 나의 몫이다.

온전히 책임져야 하고, 혼자서 쌓아가야 한다.

그래서 그림을 그린다는 것은 외롭다.

인간은 누구나 혼자이다.

—

Discarding, choosing,

and focusing are also necessary for the painting.

What to throw away, what to focus on,

and what to choose.

Those are my parts.

You have to be fully accountable and build it up by yourself.

So, painting is not lonely work.

Human beings are all alone.

69 | Healing 46 x 53cm Acrylic on canvas. 2012

70 | Healing 61 x 73cm Mixed media on canvas. 2012

'쉼'

세상은 매일, 매 순간 바쁘게 움직인다.

쉴 시간을 아껴가며 일하고,

잘 시간을 아껴가며 일한다.

때로는 쉬어갈 줄 알아야 한다.

적극적인 휴식, 때로는 바보같이 쉬어 보자.

바보같이 쉰다고 바보가 되는 것은 아니다.

바보같이 쉬는 것. 그게 진정한 '쉼'이다.

진정한 '쉼'을 취할 때, 우리는 한 발짝 더 앞으로 나아갈 수 있다.

—

'Resting'
The world moves busy every day and every moment.
I spare time to rest to work.
I spare time to sleep to work.
Sometimes, we need to know how to take a break.
Let's have a positive rest.
Just have much rest like a fool from time to time.
It will not make you stupid to be a fool.
A silly rest! That is a true 'rest'.
When we take complete "rest", we can go one step further.

PART 3

"예술의 궁극적인 목적은 치유"
"The ultimate purpose of art is healing."

71 | Healing 91 x 112cm Mixed media on canvas. 2012

이것은 내 것, 저것은 네 것.
이 사람은 내 사람, 저 사람은 적.
나누지 마라, 편 가르지 마라.
그러한 이분법에서 나오는 불안감.
그 불안감이 우리를 갉아먹는 것이다.
함께 공유하고, 함께 즐기자.
같이 나아가고, 같이 울자.
나누지 마라, 편 가르지 마라.
지긋한 이분법적 강요에서 벗어날 때
우리는 우리가 되어 함께 웃을 수 있다.

—

This is mine and that is yours.
This man is my man, the man is my enemy.
Do not divide. Do not separate.
Anxiety from such dichotomy
The anxiety is to eat us.
Share and enjoy together.
Let's go and cry together.
Do not divide and separate.
When escaping from deliberate dichotomy,
we can be together and laugh.

72 | Healing 73 x 60cm Mixed media on canvas. 2014

우리는 매일 맛보고, 냄새 맡고, 만져본다.

그것들로부터 빠르게 오는 것들만을 믿고 따른다.

자연스럽게 우리 안에 스며드는 것이다.

그러지 마라. 보이는 대로 믿지 마라.

천천히 느끼고, 곰곰이 생각하자.

현혹되지 말자.

—

We taste, smell, and touch every day.

I believe only what comes quickly from them.

It naturally penetrates into us.

Don't do that. Do not believe what you see.

Let's try to feel them with time and ponder.

Let's not be deceived.

73 | Untitled 100 x 100cm Mixed media on canvas. 2012

73
—

삶은 이야기들로 구성되어 있다.

수많은 이야기들이 서로 얽혀 있고, 단단하게 묶여 있다.

우리는 그것을 수없이 표현해 낸다.

때로는 색감으로, 때로는 음악으로, 때로는 맛으로.

그 이야기들과 부대끼고 동고동락하며 살아갈 때,

나라는 큰 맥락이 완성되어 간다.

—

Life is made up of stories.

Numerous stories are intertwined and tightly bound.

We express it countlessly.

Sometimes with colors, sometimes with music,

and sometimes with tastes.

When we live with the stories through conflicts and harmonies,

a great context, 'I' get to be completed.

74
—

예술은 자기 자신을 깎아 누적시키는 일이다.

실질적인 신체든, 자신의 감정이든, 영혼이든.

그렇게 누적되고 고인 예술은 그 자체로 빛나서

보는 이로 하여금 말간 감동을 느끼게 한다.

싱그럽게 흐르는 피로써, 빛나는 영혼으로써.

—

Art is sharing and accumulating one's ideas and feelings.

Whether it is real body, your feelings, or your soul.

Such an accumulated art within shines by themselves.

It makes the viewers touched and moved.

As fresh life and luminous soul.

74 | Healing 73 x 61cm Mixed media on canvas. 2016

75 | Healign 73 x 61cm Mixed media on canvas. 2014

75

앞만 보고 쉼 없이 달려가다가 뒤를 돌아봤을 때,

지나온 거리가 까마득히 보일 때가 있다.

지나온 거리의 풍경이나 향기 따위는

기억에 남아 있지 않다.

오로지 먼 산만을 쫓아왔으나,

먼 산은 전혀 가까워지지 않았다.

조금은 천천히 뛰어도 된다.

사뿐사뿐 걸어가도 된다.

한 발 한 발 천천히, 봄 냄새,

가을 냄새 놓치지 말고.

한 장 한 장 천천히,

중요한 부분에는 책갈피도 끼워가면서.

먼 곳만 바라보다 가까운 것을 놓치지 말자.

—

When I looked forward and I ran without rest,

there are times when the streets

that I have passed seem too far-off.

The scenery and scent of

the streets passed are not memorable.

I came only after distant mountains

but the distant mountains did not come near at all.

I can run a little slowly.

I can walk softly.

Do not miss each step.

Do not miss smell of spring and autumn.

Slowly one by one,

inserting bookmarks in important parts.

Let's not miss something closer to the far end.

76 | Healing 162 x 130cm Acrylic on canvas. 2015

절제된 아름다움.

숭고함, 장엄함, 바이올린의 선율.

첼로, 그 선율로부터 뿜어져 나오는 중후함.

이런 느낌을 한번 가져보라.

그림을 보면서, 이런 느낌을 한번 가져보자.

명랑한 재잘거림, 따뜻한 오후의 차 한잔…

—

Controlled beauty.

Melody of sublimity, gloriousness, and violin.

Cello, seriousness coming from the melody.

Try to feel such feelings.

Try to have such feelings, looking at the paintings.

Bright chatting, a cup of tea in warm afternoon…

77 | Healing 100 x 100cm Acrylic on canvas. 2015

77
—

그리움은 시간을 견디는 것이다.
찬란한 아름다움을 위하여

—

A longing is to endure time.
For brilliant beauty

78 | Healing 162 x 130cm Acrylic on canvas. 2015

감수성 회복.

때로는 미친 듯이 울어보자.

감정의 찌꺼기를 다 쏟아내 보자.

저 아래에 있는 무의식까지 쏟아내다 보면

슬금슬금 희망이 올라오는 게 느껴질 것이다.

영혼의 치유… 나는 그림을 그리다가 자주 눈물이 쏟아진다.

왠지 모를 서러움에 북받쳐서.

—

Recovery of sensitivity.

Sometimes let's cry crazy.

Let's pour out all the remnants of emotion.

If you pour the unconscious down there

You will feel a sense of hope rising up.

Healing the soul… I often pour tears as I draw the paintings.

I can not help but crying and wonder why.

79 | White & White 130 x 40cm Acrylic on canvas. 2010

79

내려놓아라.

분석하지 마라.

눈이 아닌 마음으로 볼 때 진정한 '봄'이 완성된다.

너무 많은 생각은 위험하다.

편견으로 선을 가르지 말고

있는 그대로 보되, 마음속에 당신만의 그림을 그려라.

그러할 때 당신은 똑바로 볼 수 있다.

—

Put it down.

Do not analyze.

True 'spring' is completed when we look by our mind,

not by our eyes.

Too much thinking is dangerous.

Do not divide it with prejudice.

See it as it is. Draw your own picture in your mind.

Then, you can see straightly.

80 | Untitled 130 x 40cm Acrylic on canvas. 2010

80
—

비가 오고 난 다음 숲에서 부는 바람은 박하 향이 난다.

숲은 그대로인 듯하나 순간순간 달라지는 스펙트럼…

연약한 연둣빛 이파리가 초록으로 변화되는 황홀한 경험

숲에서 바람 냄새가 난다.

—

After rain, the wind blowing from the forest smells minty.

The forest seems to be the same,

but the spectrum that changes every moment...

Enchanted experience where fragile leaves turn into green

Smell of the wind comes from the forest.

충분히 넘어지고, 충분히 울자.

또 충분히 고통받고, 충분히 다치자.

성공은 한 번의 노력만으로 성취되는 것이 아니다.

그간의 상처와 눈물, 노력.

봄은 결코 그냥 오지 않는다.

—

Let's fall down enough and cry enough.

Let's suffer enough and get hurt enough.

Success is not something which can be achieved with only one effort.

Hurt, tears, and effort meantime.

Spring doesn't come alone.

81 | Healing 53 x 46cm Mixed media on canvas. 2012

82 | Healing 73 x 64cm Acrylic on canvas. 2015

82
—

마음이 아프면 무슨 색으로 치유를 받아야 할까?
나는 마음이 복잡한 날은 그냥 영화관으로 달려간다.
어떤 영화를 보게 되더라도…
시끌시끌했던 마음에 조금의 위안을 받고 다시 작업실로 돌아온다.
영화, 나를 치유해 주는 멋진 친구.
잊을 수 없는 하이데라바드의 영화관.

—

What colors can cure our minds?
I run into a movie theater on a complex day.
No matter what movie you see…
I feel a little relieved in my mind
and return back to my workplace again.
A movie, a wonderful friend who heals me.
Unforgettable cinema of Hyderabad.

83 | Healing 91 x 73cm Mixed media on canvas. 2015

나는 예술의 역할과 필요성은 바로

삶을 좀 더 가치 있고 행복하게,

생각을 끄집어낼 수 있도록 훈련하는 것.

생각의 우물에서 물을 긷는 작업.

그것이 예술의 역할이라고 생각한다.

우리에게 행복의 원천을 제시하며

사람답게 살 수 있도록 하는 것.

—

The role and necessity of art

is to train life more valuable and happy.

It is to train to draw our ideas and thoughts out.

The work of drawing water from a well of thoughts

I think that is the role of art.

Something presenting a source of happiness

and making us live worthy of the name of men.

84 | Healing 73 x 61cm Acrylic on canvas, 2012

맑게 갠 날. 가볍게 산책하듯어.
그렇게 살아가자.

—

On certain clear day, like a light walk.
Let's live like that.

85 | Untitled 73 x 61cm Mixed media on canvas. 2015

오래된 진공관 라디오.

친구가 생일 선물로 나에게 주었던 잊을 수 없는 선물.

지금도 작업실에서 내 곁을 묵묵히 지키고 있다.

디지털의 깨끗한 소리보다 인간적인 느낌이 있다.

소리에서 사람 냄새가 난다.

—

Old vacuum tube, radio.

An unforgettable gift that my friend gave me as a birthday present.

I still keep it my side silently in studio.

It keeps more human feelings than the clear sound of digital.

The sound smells of people.

86 | Healing 194 x 260cm Mixed media on canvas. 2014

음악도 색채가 있다.

한때 미친 듯이 들었던 탱고의 음악들도 지금은 시들해졌다.

탱고의 색은 무슨 색이었을까?

사람의 땀 냄새가 범벅된 색은…?

작업을 하다 보면

비가 오고, 바람이 불고, 때로는 맑은 날도 있듯이,

미친 듯이 좋아하던 음악이 시들해지고

미친 듯이 좋아하던 색이 시들해질 때도 있다.

새로움이 들어와야 한다.

—

Music also has colors.

Tango music which I have heard once crazy has faded now.

What was the color of Tango?

The color of people's sweat is?

While I work,

like it sometimes rains, wind blows,

and some clear days come too,

my crazy favorite music is fading away.

The colors that I liked like crazy are sometimes fading away.

Newness needs to come.

87 | White & White 163 x 130cm Mixed media on canvas. 2006

무심함.

화려하지 않은 무심함.

깊이 있게 보아야만 찾을 수 있다.

무심한 그림의 숨은 매력을…

그래서 눈으로만 보아서는 전체를 볼 수 없다.

마음, 그리고 오감으로 바라보자.

—

Indifference.

Indifference not so gorgeous.

You can find it only when you look at it to the deep.

The hidden charms of the indifferent paintings…

So, I can not see the whole thing just by your eyes.

With your mind, try to look at it with your five senses.

포도를 따서 발로 으깨고 그 즙을 숙성시켜서,

5년이 지나 거르고 걸러야 와인이 된다.

한 방울의 맛있는 와인이 될 때까지 응축이 되어야 하는 것이다.

작업도 응축되는 시간이 필요하다.

—

Picking up the grapes, crushing them with feet, ripening its juice

Five years later, the wine can be ready through filtering.

It should be condensed until it becomes a drop of delicious wine.

The work also needs time to be condensed.

88 | Healing 194 x 260cm Mixed media on canvas. 2015

89 | Healing 73 x 61cm Mixed media on canvas. 2015

89

우리는 책을 보며 그 책의 내용에 대해 생각한다.

종이 위에 펼쳐져 있는 글자들을 그대로 따라가는 것이다.

다르게 생각해 보자,

또 그 '다름에 대한 생각'에 대해서 생각해 보자.

대체 무엇이 다른 것인지.

대체 어떻게 다르게 생각하는지.

—

We read books and think of the meaning of the books.

We follow the letters spread on the papers as they are.

Let's try to think differently.

Let's think about the idea of difference.

What is different.

How different.

90 | Healing 73 x 61cm Mixed media on canvas. 2015

우리 모두는 삶이라는 흙 속에서

저마다의 꽃을 피워내기 위해서 끊임없이 노력한다.

때로는 흙 표면으로 보이는 것에만 끝없이 치중한다.

하지만 꽃은, 표면을 가꾸는 것만으로는 피어나지 않는다.

꽃은 보이지 않는 뿌리로부터 피어나는 것이다.

작업도 삶과 마찬가지이다.

오로지 한길로 끊임없이 가야만

꽃을 피울 수 있다고 나는 생각한다.

—

We all live on the soil, called 'lives'.

We try hard endlessly to bloom our own flowers on it.

We sometimes focused on what appears on the surface of the soil.

Flowers, however, do not bloom only by cultivating their surfaces.

Flowers bloom from invisible roots.

Work is the same as life.

When I go to one way enough continuously,

I think I can bloom.

우리는 살아가며 수많은 일들을 겪는다.

때로는 힘들고 슬픈 일들을, 때로는 찬란하게 밝은 기쁜 일들을.

우리는 그 모든 일들을 좋고 나쁜 일들로 나누며, 가치를 매긴다.

이 일은 나에게 해가 되는 나쁜 일.

저 일은 나를 살아 숨 쉬게 하는 기쁜 일.

하지만 일의 가치를 판단하는 것은, 다름 아닌 나 자신의 마음이다.

나의 태도에 따라서 좋은 일도 나쁜 일이 될 수 있고,

나쁜 일도 좋은 일이 될 수 있다.

똑같은 일을 하더라도 어떤 마음가짐으로 임하는지가 중요한 것이다.

—

We live and suffer numerous things.

Sometimes difficult and sad things, sometimes brilliant and bright things.

We try to divide all such things into good and bad ones.

And we try to value them.

This is a bad thing to me. That work is a joy that makes me breathe.

But it is my own mind that judges the value of works.

Depending on my attitudes, even good things can be bad.

Bad things can be good things.

Even if you do the same works, it is important with which attitude you focus on it.

92 | White & White 130 x 40cm Acrylic on canvas. 2006

92

끊임없이 반복되는 공간감.

그리고 지우고 그리고 지우고…

반복되는 과정 속에서 나는 본질을 생각한다.

작업의 본질.

지우는 것과 남겨놓는 것.

그 속에 응축된 시간들…

내 작업의 본질.

—

Constantly repeating the sense of space

And erasing, erasing...

I think of the essence in the process of repeating.

The essence of works.

Erasing and leaving.

Time condensed in it...

The essence of my works.

93 | Healing 73 x 61cm Acrylic on canvas. 2006

정적.

아무것도 들여놓지 않고 싶은 마음.

때로는 음악도 원치 않는다.

그냥 비워 버리고 싶은 것이다.

그냥, 모든 것을.

—

Silence.

Mind where I don't want to let anything in

Sometimes I do not want music, either.

I just want to leave it empty.

Just, everything.

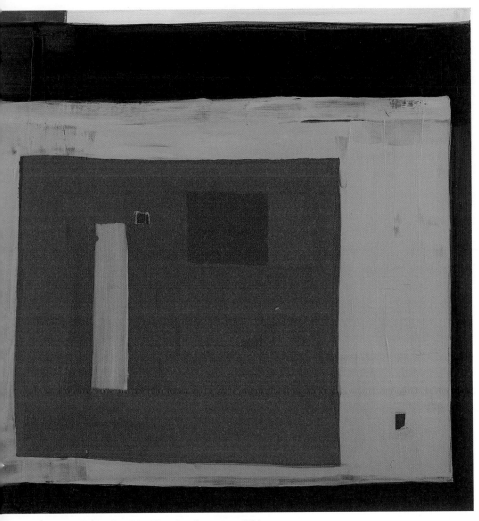

94 | Healing 100 x 100cm Acrylic on canvas. 2015

바람 소리를 듣다 보면,

미세하게 여름이 다르고

봄이 다르며 겨울이 다르다.

진동의 느낌이 다르며, 울림의 깊이 또한 다르다.

가만히 귀 기울여 들어봐야 들을 수 있다.

사람의 마음 또한 가만히 귀 기울여 들어봐야만 알 수 있다.

—

When you hear the wind,

Summer is approaching minutely.

The spring is different and the winter is different.

The feeling of vibration is different

and the depth of resonance is also different.

Only when we listen carefully, we can listen.

The mind of a person can also be known only by listening carefully.

하루에 한 번씩 내 안의 나에게 말을 걸어본다.

너는 지금 어디에 머무르고 있는지.

—

I talk to myself in me once a day.

Where I am staying now.

95 | Healing 73 x 61cm Acrylic on canvas. 2015

96 | Saekdong 100 x 100cm Acrylic on canvas. 2010

사람들은 단순하게, 붓을 들고 물감을 찍어서
그림을 그리면 된다고 생각한다.
하지만 단순히 겉을 그려낸다고 해서 되는 것이 아니다.
그림을 그린다는 것은 모든 감정을 녹여내어 영혼을 만나는 것이다.

—

People simply think that it is fine to paint their brushes with paints.
However, it does not mean simply drawing the outside.
Painting is something to melt all the emotions
and meet the souls.

97 | Untitled 163 x 130cm Mixed media on canvas. 2012

붓을 들 때는,
이미 머릿속에서 그림을 다 그렸을 때인데
그리고 나서도 계속
허공에 붓질하는 느낌이 들 때가 있다.

그러다가 단 한 점.
가슴에 남는 그림 단 한 점만 나와도
기쁨이 내 영혼 속으로 채워져 올라온다.

—

When I hold a brush is the time when

I already painted the picture in my mind.

And then continuously,

I feel like I'm brushing in the air.

Meanwhile, a single piece,

only by one single piece of painting staying in my mind,

a great joy is filled up in my soul and rises.

98
—

색은 치유의 힘이 있다.

그래서 밝고 경쾌하며 발랄한 느낌의 그림을 보면

마음이 따뜻해지곤 한다.

거침없는 표현, 하지만 때로는 서툰 듯이.

그저 손이 가는 대로 경쾌하게.

형광색들이 벌이는 불꽃축제처럼

그렇게 화면을 장식하고 싶다.

—

Colors have the power of healing.

So, when I look at the painting

that is bright, light, and sporty,

I feel warm.

Unstoppable expressions but sometimes they sound rough.

Just as your hands go, merrily

like a fireworks festival with fluorescent colors playing

I want to decorate the image in the way.

Saekdong 100 x 100cm Mixed media on canvas. 2010

물빛은 표현하기가 쉽지 않다.

단순한 파란색이 아니다.

햇빛의 느낌, 바람, 시간, 모든 것들이 색을 만들어 낸다.

시시때때로 바뀌는 색.

눈으로만 보면 알 수 없다.

미세한 떨림을 어찌 알 수 있겠는가.

체험해 봐야 한다.

그 체험은 시간이 걸린다.

절대로 한 번에 알 수가 없기 때문이다.

—

Water light is not easy to express.

It's not just blue.

The feeling of sunshine, wind, time, and everything create colors.

The colors changing occasionally.

We can not tell just by our eyes.

How can we know the slightest trembling?

We need to experience.

The experience takes time.

It is because we can not tell at once.

100 | Saekdong 100 x 100cm Acrylic on canvas. 2010

그림을 그리는 것 자체가

나의 영혼을 치유하는 것이며,

그림을 보는 것 자체가

이미 치유를 받는 것이다.

나의 그림을 통해서

이 느낌과 창조적인 상상을 전해 주고 싶다.

—

The painting itself is
healing my soul.
Looking at the paintings itself
is already being healed.
Through my paintings,
I want to deliver this feeling and creative imagination.

101 | Untitled 73 x 61cm Acrylic on canvas. 2015

101

공간의 단절이 필요하다.

떠나봐야 보이는 것처럼,

소중한 느낌도

소중한 공간도

소중한 관계도

공간의 이동이 있어야 새로워진다.

그래서 작업실이 세계에 세 군데만 있었으면…

나는 희망 한다.

—

We need a break in space.

As we can see, only when we leave

precious feeling,

important space, and

precious relationship

these can be fresh only in different spaces in different places.

So, I wish to have three studio in the world…

102

작업실에서는 창밖을 볼 수 없다.

창은 있으나, 그냥 막아 버렸다.

이곳에 있으면 눈이 오는지, 비가 오는지…

어떤 때는 그냥 소리로 직감할 뿐이다.

막혀 있지만, 동시에 완전히 열려 있는 공간이기도 하다.

열림과 닫힘의 차이는 그저 마음의 차이이다.

그림 속에 열려 있는 공간을 만들고 싶다.

—

I can not see outside from the window in studio.

It has windows. But I just blocked them.

When I am here, I can sense only by sound.

It doesn't matter if it is snowing, raining…

Sometimes I can sense it just by sound.

It is blocked but completely open space at the same time.

The difference between opening

and closing is just a difference in mind.

I would like to create an open space in the painting.

102 | Healing 73 x 61cm Acrylic on canvas. 2015

103 | 01:30am at Hyderabad Airport 73 x 61cm Acrylic on canvas. 2016

103

행복한 슬픔.

사랑은 슬픔을 기다리고, 즐기는 것이다.

좋은 그림 또한 기다려야만 한다.

정직한 시간과 땀으로써.

어쩌면 작업은 행복한 슬픔을 견디는 것이다.

꽃이 필 때까지, 좋은 작품 그 한 점을 위하여…

—

Happy sadness.

Love is waiting for sadness and enjoying.

Good paintings, we need to wait

with honest time and sweat.

Maybe, work is to endure happy sadness.

Until flowers bloom for a good piece of work...

EPILOGUE

3주일을,

책을 마무리하지 못하고 있는데,

봄이 왔다. 봄은 희망이고 그리움이다.

지금 생각해 봐도, 영원히 책을 쓰지 못할 것 같았다.

그냥 언제나 그랬듯이 묵묵히 가보자.

모든 시작이 무모하듯이.

책을 마무리하고 나니, 부족함으로 부끄러움이 앞선다.

그러나 그 부끄러움이 새로운 나를 발견해 나가는 과정이라면

겸허하게 부끄러움을 받아들이고 싶다.

봄날, 바람이 달다.

― 새벽 작업실에서 **서정자**

For three weeks,

while I couldn't have finished the book,

spring comes. Spring is hope and longing.

Thinking of the day, I felt I could not write a book forever.

Let's go forward silently as usual.

Like all the beginnings are reckless.

After finishing my book, my inadequacy leads me to feel shameful.

However, if that shame is a process of discovering me,

I want to embrace the shame humbly.

One spring day, the wind is sweet.

- **Seo Jeong-Ja** in studio at dawn

ART IS LIFE
바람이 달다

초판 1쇄   2017년 05월 15일

지은이   서정자
발행인   김재홍
편집장   김옥경
디자인   이유정, 이슬기
마케팅   이연실

발행처   도서출판 지식공감
등록번호   제396-2012-000018호
주소   경기도 고양시 일산동구 견달산로225번길 112
전화   02-3141-2700
팩스   02-322-3089
홈페이지   www.bookdaum.com

가격   16,000원
ISBN   979-11-5622-277-4 03810

CIP제어번호   CIP2017007383
이 도서의 국립중앙도서관 출판도서목록(CIP)은 서지정보유통지원시스템 홈페이지
(http://seoji.nl.go.kr)와 국가자료공동목록시스템(http://www.nl.go.kr/kolisnet)에서
이용하실 수 있습니다.